# TRACKER

John Borne always looked forward to deer hunting—
not the killing part, but the time spent with his
grandfather in the vast swamp bogs near their farm.
John loved the way the old man had with the woods,
loved the way he saw life. For them, the taking of a
deer was a necessity, not sport—it meant meat on the
table during the long Minnesota winter.

But everything is changed now. His grandfather is
dying of cancer, and John, thirteen, will hunt alone
this year.

A few nights before the opening of the season, a doe
appears to him by the side of the barn. She doesn't
run. She waits, watching. There is something about
her that John *recognizes*. And so, on the first morning, John sets off seeking not just a deer but a more
elusive quarry—a peace with death. He sees the doe
again and knows that wherever the trail leads, wherever she beckons, he will follow to the end.

*Also by Gary Paulsen*

# TRACKER

✝✝✝✝✝✝✝✝✝✝✝✝✝✝✝✝✝✝✝✝✝✝✝✝✝✝✝✝✝✝✝✝✝✝✝✝✝✝✝✝✝✝

## BY GARY PAULSEN

## SCHOLASTIC INC.
New York  Toronto  London  Auckland  Sydney
Mexico City  New Delhi  Hong Kong  Buenos Aires

ISBN 0-590-44098-5

62                                          20 21 22 23 24 25 26/0

Printed in the U.S.A.                          40

The text of this book was set in 11-point Aster.

*To Nancy Polette,*
*who earned it*

# TRACKER

# ONE

John Borne sat at the breakfast table and tried to see the look of death on his grandfather. He could not. If a change were there, he could not see it.

Clay Borne had ruddy cheeks, a head of white hair, clear eyes and steady hands as he buttered a great slab of fresh bread hot from the wood stove, and humor in the corners of his eyes just as he always had.

*He is life*, John thought—*not death.*

*He will never be death. Whenever I turn around and need him, Grandpa will be there.*

But that's not what the doctors said. Two weeks ago, at the hospital in Grand Forks, the doctors had asked them to come into a small green room—or had asked his grandparents and John had gone with them because nobody said he couldn't.

"There is nothing more to do," the doctors said. They looked sad. But it was a sadness that would go away. "We can't stop the cancer."

And John had watched his grandmother sag. She made no sound but just sagged. A part of her went out at the words and she started down and John caught her on one side and his grandfather on the other and they put her in a chair.

"It will be all right," Clay told her gently. "It will be all right."

But how could it be?

The doctors had done tests and more tests and worked with chemicals and knives and finally had sent John Borne's grandfather home to die in peace on the small farm at the edge of the woods, the farm where he had been born and lived all his life, the farm where John had lived for nine years, since he was four and his parents were killed in a plane crash in the northern woods.

Home.

"You're not eating, John." His grandmother turned from the stove. "Cold breakfast sits hard, and a hard breakfast won't warm you on a snowy morning."

He nodded and put food in his mouth but tasted nothing, felt only the texture of the eggs and crumbled bacon. His grandmother talked like that, as though she were just about to break into poetry. When John listened to her for a while he caught himself expecting things to rhyme but they never quite did.

She had cried for a time, for days, but she was through with that now just as John had cried but was through with it now. Crying changed nothing.

There was still the fact that the doctors said his grandfather had only a few months to live and so John had tried to see the look of death on him but could not.

He had seen it on many things. They lived close to the land and made all their own meat, and to make meat it was necessary to make death. He had helped his grandfather slaughter cattle and seen death there, and once on a man, the farmer who had lived next door. His tractor had backed over him and John had been the one to find the body when he went to deliver eggs and there had been death on the ground.

But it wasn't here now.

There wasn't the looseness of death or the hot-sweet smell of it or even the tiredness of it. There was no change in his grandfather, no change at all. He kept right on working and carving the little woodcarvings in the kitchen at night and laughing and playing small jokes and eating well and looking to the next day. Always looking to the next day.

His grandfather glanced up from his plate suddenly, his fork halfway to his mouth. "Isn't the food good enough for you?"

John had stopped eating again without knowing it. "Of course . . ." He took another mouthful.

"There's an inch of snow out there." The old man chewed slowly and carefully. "Deer season starts Saturday. The snow will be good for tracking."

They hunted deer every year and normally John would start getting excited two or three days before season. He'd clean and reclean his rifle, look more and more to the woods and start losing sleep. This year was different. Normally they would get up at three in the morning and do chores and the milking so they could be in the woods by first gray light; and they would do that for the entire two weeks of deer season or until they got a deer. But this year that was all changed.

His grandfather wasn't going to hunt this year. "I'll stay home and do the chores," he'd said one morning, sitting in the yellow glow of the kerosene lamp on the kitchen table, his hands folded in front of him on the oilcloth. "It's time you hunted alone."

And John had nodded but it had been wrong, too wrong. They always hunted together, they always did everything together.

John had started hunting deer when he was ten, first without a gun, just going with his grandfather. Then when he was eleven he took a shotgun and got his first deer and he had taken deer every season since, using a rifle after the first year. He was now thirteen.

Three deer he had taken with his grandfather, hunting the cold crisp mornings in November, hunting down the long cold trails in the swamps in the new snow. Three times he had given death to the deer, seen the new blood on the snow, seen the look of death . . .

He stopped thinking, concentrated on eating the pancakes his grandmother had put in front of him. But it was impossible to keep the memories out. *Things don't change*, he thought. *People don't die. They couldn't* . . . It was always somebody else who died, never people you were close to. Even though his parents had gone down in a plane crash and were surely dead, it had happened when he was very young and so he didn't know them. He had not seen the change brought by death—the change that was supposed to come but, for John, never did.

But for his grandfather to stay home from hunting deer—that was too much. Too much of a change. It was like admitting that death was coming.

He got the last of the pancakes down. They tasted like sticky wood. Then he took his plate to the sink and used the hand pump to rinse the syrup down the drain.

"I'll go do chores," he said, turning from the pump, looking at his grandfather at the table but still not looking, saying but not saying. *I'll go do chores and you can't die*, he thought, a scream in his mind. "I'll go start milking."

His grandfather nodded. "I'll be out in a minute, after I finish my coffee."

And that wasn't a change. He always hung back and had coffee with Agatha, John's grandmother. They sat in the morning dark, in the yellow of the lamp, and sipped coffee and talked about what the day might bring and at least that hadn't changed.

John threw his chores jacket with all the holes over his shirt and pulled on the rubber barn boots and went outside into the cold, crunching in the new snow. His breath made small puffs, led the way to the warm smells of the barn.

Once he was out of the house in the dark of the morning he could use his mind to make things all right. It was still a cold clear morning, he was still going to milk the cows and clean the barn and feed and water the stock, still going to smell and feel the heat of the barn.

Those things hadn't changed and so maybe the other thing wouldn't change, maybe the doctors were wrong. They were just people. They could be wrong.

He kicked the ice from the barn door and went in, swinging the door wide and brushing the new snow back. letting his spirits come up.

It was impossible to feel bad when you entered

a barn in the winter where the cows were waiting to be fed; impossible to be sad when there was work to do.

He started chores.

# TWO

His grandfather did not come out to help with chores and John did them alone.

He didn't mind. It had happened before many times and in some ways he liked it. During the week, the school bus came before chores were finished and John had to leave the farm then. He always felt as if he were missing something. Now that it was Sunday he did not have to leave and so he could work morning chores all the way to done. That's how his grandfather always talked about work—you didn't just work so many hours or days. You worked a job to done. All the way to done. No matter how long it took.

And chores, morning chores, milking, and cleaning the barn and feeding calves and pigs and chickens was work but more, too. There was something about it that lifted it above work for John.

At school his best friend was a boy named Emil Peterson and Emil thought he was crazy to like chores.

"That's just hard work, that's all it is," he'd told John more than once. Emil hated chores at his own place, or anyplace else for that matter. "You think it's fun to slop around in cow crap all morning? You're crazy."

John had tried to explain but nothing had come out right. Chores was the first thing of the day, it was the new thing of each day and it was work but it touched something else in his mind, touched a place that made him think of good things, of growing and rich things.

More than once in the winter he had come into

the barn only to stop just inside the door and listen and smell and feel the richness of it. The stink of the manure was even rich, and the rumbling of the cows' stomachs in the dark, the fresh warm smell of them just after he came in from the bitter cold, the sound of their teeth as they chewed their cuds, the quiet grunts and chuckles that came from the horses in the stalls at the end . . .

"It's gentle," he'd tried to tell Emil. "Gentle and right, somehow. The feeling of the barn in the morning."

But Emil hadn't agreed and John hadn't brought it up again because when somebody doesn't want to see a thing you can't make him see it.

His grandfather had fought the Japanese in World War II and had been wounded and later had been in the occupying force in Japan, and the hating part of war had gone and he had come to love them. That's how he put it, talking to John one morning during the morning lunch break.

"I came to love them and the beauty they see in things and the way they see the beauty. They look for small beauty, look for the beauty in even ugly things, and they compose songs and poetry to celebrate that beauty. Whole poems have been written about a single petal on a flower. One tear on a child's cheek."

And in a way that was what morning chores were for John—a whole series of small beauties. All the sounds and smells and feelings came as separate little bursts of beauty and he found himself making small poems in his mind while he did even the dirtiest work.

*The cows greet*
*gently.*
*On a cold morning.*

The words went through his head while he was taking the manure fork and sweeping it down the gutter to clean the night's mess and he decided he would tell them to his grandfather when he came out.

The ritual of chores was always the same, at least in the fall and winter when the cows were kept in: clean the gutters, feed hay, feed silage— the warm rich smell of the hot corn from the silo always made his mouth water—and milk. There were seventeen milk cows and four about to come in to milk season and when the milking was done it was time to feed milk to the calves in buckets and separate the rest of the milk and cream in the separator.

John could have done it with his eyes closed by the time he was twelve. At thirteen it was so automatic that he didn't have to use his mind at all and could think of other things.

He brought the milk stool from where it hung and settled in alongside Eunice, the first cow, and nestled his head in her flank and began pulling milk into the bucket with a hissy tingling foamy sound.

*Don't watch the milk*, he thought. After you'd been milking for a while you learned to not watch the milk, because it came in a small stream and never seemed to fill the bucket if you watched it. But if you looked away for a time and then looked back, the level in the bucket would have come up, and he wondered while he milked how many other things were like that. Wondered if there were many parts of living that only changed when you looked away and looked back.

*Like Grandpa.*

It came in like a hot worm, the thought — like a needle in a blister. He didn't want to think of his grandfather. Not now, not yet. There would be time for that later, too much time for that later.

But it came. He couldn't stop it. The thought slid in the side and with it a small hope.

*If I don't see what is happening to him*, the hope said, *then it isn't happening.*

*It's the opposite of filling the bucket with milk. If I watch him all the time I won't see the change that death is bringing and so it can't be.*

*Can't be.*

Death couldn't come if you were watching for it.

John went to the next cow, Marge, a big Holstein who was an easy milker because she dropped the milk as soon as you started pulling.

The ritual again. The foamy hiss of the milk, the head cradled in the flank of the cow, the warm-sweet smell of milk coming up and the thinking.

The thinking came again. There was school tomorrow, school all week and then deer season would start. He would think about that: getting through school all week and going deer hunting.

If he worked at that the other thing wouldn't come in. If he kept his mind going on school and going deer hunting . . .

School was a strange time for John. He was pretty much a loner, except for his best friend Emil, and he didn't get the entertainment part of school at all.

He approached school like a job—work to do. Something that had to get done, like chores. Usually he brought none of his home life to school and very little school came home.

But he did talk to Emil about his grandfather. The pressure had been too great—a building, blinding thing—and he had told Emil about it last week by their lockers.

All around was noise, kids moving, hall traffic with teachers watching.

"He's going to die," John had said.

"What?" Emil slammed his locker. It wouldn't catch any other way.

"Grandpa's going to die," John repeated, slightly louder. "Of cancer."

Emil looked directly into his eyes. "That's not fair. He's too good. Too good for dying."

"Just the same," John said, starting to cry. "Just the same—the doctors said."

"That doesn't make it fair."

And Emil was right. It wasn't fair.

He thought suddenly of the deer he had killed.

Three of them. The first one a doe, then a buck and a doe, and he had killed them all.

Jolts of noise and violence—that's what he remembered—the slam of the shotgun as it recoiled into his shoulder, the flat-crack of the bullet leaving the barrel, the second that hung forever in his mind as he saw the bullet hit the deer just in back of the shoulder, the hair and blood that flew with the bullet and the deer staggering sideways with the shock of being hit.

Sideways and down, he remembered, and the eyes looking, always looking for what had happened, looking in confusion and pain and finally clouding as death came; clouding and filming over with death.

The first deer.

And the thought crept in that maybe the deer had been good, just as his grandfather was good, and maybe it wasn't fair for the deer, either.

The second deer had been worse. The bullet had taken it too far back, in the lungs, and death had come slowly and John had to shoot again to kill it and it had seen him and that bothered him.

For a time.

Then that thing happened that happens to all people who hunt, or to everybody he'd talked to about deer hunting. They were sad about it, but the sad part only lasted a short time and wore off and was replaced by a hard feeling, almost an excitement. And after that it wasn't hard to kill deer anymore, wasn't hard to give them death, and sometimes that bothered John, too. More than he admitted to other kids at school or even to his grandfather.

He wasn't sure it was right to feel that hard way about killing, about death, about shooting animals and giving them death.

He realized with a start that he was crying while he milked, the tears dropping off his cheeks into the foam of the milk at the side of the bucket, making round holes down through the foam.

He couldn't remember starting to cry, couldn't think when the great sadness came down on his shoulders, but it was there and he thought of his grandfather and the crying got worse and he buried his face in the cow's flank and ground his teeth together and made the crying stop. There would be nothing from crying, he felt—nothing to help at all from crying.

But still the sobs came, jerking his head as he milked, the tears dripping down in the foam.

# THREE

During the next week things almost went back to normal, if a bit quiet, around the house. Now and then John would catch his grandmother crying, just little tears as she worked, and once he saw his grandfather staring out the window when there was nothing to see but darkness, his hands still upon the carving he was working on. But other than that things were almost the same as always.

And in a way the week was the same as the ritual of the chores. There was getting up and working in the barn and then school, and for a change John liked school—it gave him something outside himself to think about, forced him to look away from his own life.

In the mornings at breakfast he forced himself to not stare at his grandfather and by Tuesday it was easier and he could talk without his voice catching.

They talked as if nothing were going to happen. As if things would go on and on.

"Those calves will have to come on hay in a couple of weeks, hay and a little silage, or they won't be ready for grass in the spring when we let them out," his grandfather said Wednesday morning. "We don't want them to bloat when they hit the pastures."

John nodded. "I'll see to it."

"We'll have to check the traces on the stoneboat for hauling manure out to the back forty sometime this week. If we don't I think they might break with the load and we need to get manure on top of the snow this winter so it can soak in or we won't make good corn next spring . . ."

"I'll see to it after school."

"There'll be a lot of work."

"I'll handle it."

And his grandfather had gone back to carving the small figures, the way it had always been. In the evenings they would sit in the kitchen and take heat from the kitchen wood stove and his grandfather would carve little horses and men from the old logging days and talk of all the work that had to be done and John would nod and smile and eat pie and drink cold milk from the well house and finally go to sleep, right at the table if he didn't catch himself.

The work went on. After school there was a small amount of homework and then the work of the farm. John fixed the stoneboat traces, put new boards in the workhorse stalls where the team had cribbed the old ones, drained the tractor for winter, sealed the granary to hold the harvest. The work went on. It fed on itself so that work made more work.

Once the stoneboat traces were fixed it was necessary to use the stoneboat to clean out the large manure pile behind the barn and that meant using the two horses and *that* meant still more work.

"They call them workhorses because it's a lot

of work to use them," his grandfather said almost every time they harnessed the team. "But it's a good work, a full work. And they always start up in the winter, horses do—always. Not like tractors in the cold."

John liked using the team, even with the extra work. The horses were huge and immensely strong and yet full of a kind of gentle courtesy, a slow thoughtfulness that made them better than a tractor.

When he harnessed them they stood to the collar and put their heads in and made it easy for him to reach up and around and to throw the harnesses over their backs. They were named Jim and Lars and they were both brown and had white blazes on their faces, but they had different minds. Jim would stand tight in the harness, leaning forward slightly against the load, while Lars stood easy and relaxed and jerked out when told to get up.

John hauled manure for three nights after chores, late into the night. The work kept him from thinking. When milking was done, his grandfather would help him harness and he would use the fork to load the stoneboat from the manure pile in back of the barn, then stand in front of the load on the planking while the horses took the stoneboat out to the field.

They had been doing it so long that he could leave the reins tied to the rein bracket in front. They knew where to go and what had to be done when they got the load out there, and John stood leaning against the fork in the darkness while the steel runners crunched through the shallow snow.

It was cold, November cold when the body isn't used to it yet, and he wore his heavy chores jacket, so when he got to the field he had to take it off because it would be too warm when he started to fork the manure off. And it was while he was taking his coat off Wednesday night that he saw the deer.

The horses were standing in their own steam and he had jammed the fork down in the manure and pulled one arm out of his jacket sleeve and turned in the moonlight—and there she stood.

It was a doe, a small one—he could tell by her neck and lack of antlers. She wasn't thirty feet away to his right rear.

Deer often came out to check the manure, that wasn't unusual. There were seeds which passed through the cows and horses, and after snow the deer had to work a little harder for food, so the seeds were easy picking.

Many times in the past John had seen deer working through the clumps of manure. But this one was different.

She stood and stared at him for what seemed like hours, stood with little puffs of steam coming out of her nostrils in the moonlight, flaring to smell him, and didn't run.

Usually when deer separated the man from the horse smell they ran—man killed, man was the death smell.

But she stood, stood as if waiting for something, and John hung with one sleeve off and one on and stared at her, saw every part of her, saw her ears flick and her eyes move and then she was gone—gone so fast that she might not ever have been there.

But she left something in John, a picture of beauty that hung in his mind the way a picture will sometimes stay in your eyes when you close them, burned in.

The horses took the stoneboat down the field and he threw the manure off to each side, a fork left and a fork right, and still the picture was in his thoughts, and on the way home, the quarter mile back to the barn, he realized that the only way he could make the picture whole would be to compose a poem about it, the way his grandfather said the Japanese did.

> *The doe stood*
> *in puffs of steam*
> > *waiting.*

Later that night in the kitchen after supper he told his grandfather about it, about the way the deer stood and the beauty of it and the poem he had composed.

"A rare moment," Clay said. "But the poem only has partial meaning for me. What was she waiting for?"

John thought, wondering why the word had come into the poem in the first place. "I don't know."

"Sometimes the best beauty comes from that."

"From what?"

"From where you don't know, from instinct." His grandfather smiled. "The best joy and beauty are the kinds that are unplanned, and the same is true of painting or poetry. Don't chew at it too much. It's beautiful, and it makes you remember a beautiful part of your life and that's enough."

John nodded but he couldn't get her out of his mind just the same. Tired as he was, late as it was, he lay in his bed upstairs and remembered the deer and the small poem and tried to think of what she might have been waiting for—why she would have stood looking at him for so long. Especially in fall, in snow, only two days before deer season when all the deer seem to sense danger around them and get jumpy and will actually run from each other, let alone a man.

It was as if she had been waiting for him, waiting for John, standing in the moonlight against the snow, waiting for him.

But to do what?

# FOUR

Deer season.

The time for the taking of meat, the time for the giving of death to the deer for the taking of meat to get through the winter.

John did not think of hunting in the normally accepted manner. Once, a man came up from another state to go deer hunting and he talked of why he hunted.

He talked of how it made him more of a man to hunt and kill a deer. He talked of all the skill it took to kill a deer, all the knowledge it took to kill a deer.

John's grandfather would not allow the man to hunt on his land because he made deer hunting more than it should be.

"We take meat," he told John, watching the man drive away. "That's all we do—we take meat with a gun. It doesn't make you a man. It doesn't make you anything to kill. We make meat, that's all."

And that's how John thought of hunting—a way to put meat up for the winter.

After four years, the edge was largely gone from hunting, but there was still a nudge of excitement the night before season, a small thrum in the back of John's mind as he took down the rifle and began to clean it, to make sure the sights were set correctly.

He worked at the kitchen table with a small screwdriver and took the rifle apart completely and used an old toothbrush to clean each part and screw.

His grandfather carved, and drank tea and nodded approval now and then, though it wasn't required.

"If you work that swamp down to the north

early in the morning you should come on some nice bucks. Get a buck first for the tallow. You can take a doe later for good meat."

John nodded. "I thought about the swamp, but it might be a little rough going with the new snow." It was snowing outside as they talked, large flakes with almost no weight. They would make a light powder, ideal for tracking. With new snow in the morning any track John saw would be fresh. "I wish you were coming with me."

"Not this time. I'll take a year off." His grandfather's hands stopped carving for a moment and he looked out the window. "I'll pass this year—I've had plenty of hunting."

John felt his eyes moisten and fought the feeling down. "Well. I'll make meat all right but, you know, it's just more fun with you . . ."

For a time neither of them said anything and his grandmother turned from the stove where she was kneading bread on top of the water reservoir. She said nothing but looked at the table, at them, then looked back and John saw she was crying.

"Dammit. That's enough of that now. There's been enough of that damn caterwauling and carrying on around here . . ."

John was startled. Rarely did his grandfather swear, and never in the house. He put the parts of the rifle down and sat still.

"What's happening to me happens to every single human being on the face of this earth—nobody gets away from it. Nobody. So quit all this misting up and raining and let's get to the business at hand."

He sat still, very still, and stayed looking out the window—as if he might have been talking to the world, though it was dark and nothing showed but flakes now and then as they came into the glow from the table lamp.

John's grandmother looked at his back for a full ten seconds and then fled from the room crying and John waited another half a minute before picking up his rifle and starting to clean it again, though it was clean enough.

His grandfather sighed. "I didn't do that well, I'm afraid. I meant it to come out better, come out nice. But you see what I mean, don't you?"

John nodded. "Sort of. It's just that—well—you know. It's you this time, not somebody else. And when it's somebody close . . ." He let the thought trail off.

"I know. But that doesn't change anything, does

it? It still happens. That's the one fact that holds true about this sort of business, no matter what you do, you can't change it. It's coming."

*How strange it is,* John thought, *for him to talk about it this way. He's talking about his own death, his own end. The end of him.*

"When I was young I used to think it couldn't be." The old man started carving again, looking down at the wood in his hands. He was making a workhorse that would go on a small sled which he had yet to make. The chips and shavings curled off and dropped on the table and when he had a small pile of them he carefully scraped them together and got up and put them in the wood stove. Then he started carving again, gentle curves coming off the soft clear pine. "But I was wrong."

For a time there was silence, John staring down at the rifle on the table, his grandfather carving. Before they spoke again John's grandmother came back. Her eyes were moist and some hair had loosened from the gray bun at the back of her neck. She stood over the stove but there was nothing to cook and she was just waiting.

"I'm sorry, Aggie," Clay said, still carving. "Sometimes I lose control and . . . I'm sorry."

"Don't be silly."

And John thought that just then, that second, things were back to normal. He was carving and she was at the stove and there was that making-business sound in her voice, as if they had been fooling around and joking the way they sometimes did and she wanted them to stop.

"You bring the liver home when you get a deer, hear?" His grandfather looked up from the wood. "I've been thinking of fresh liver for a long time. You bring it home."

"I will." For the last two years there had been rumors circulating that deer livers were not good because they had some kind of tiny worms, and they had left the livers in the woods when they gutted the deer out. "I promise."

"Good. You take a fresh liver and fry it up with some fresh onions and some good greasy potatoes and you got a meal."

"Grease isn't good for you." Agatha turned from the sink, where she was pumping water to refill the reservoir on the stove. "Too much grease is bad."

The old man smiled. "Well. Yes. I suppose it is—but I'm not too sure it matters anymore. I think if I want to get a little greasy with my food it should be all right."

"Just the same, just the same."

"I'll get the liver," John cut in. "Don't worry. The liver and the heart. If I get a deer."

"You'll get one. You've got the touch of it. Some people hunt and hunt and never get a deer and some go out and get one every year. You'll get one just the way I always get one."

"I wish you were going out with me this year." It came without John calling for it, just slipped loose and was gone and he saw the corners of the old man's eyes tighten and he hated himself then, hated himself for the stupidity of what he had said, hated himself for causing hurt.

"I'll stay back and do the chores," his grandfather said, looking down. "This is your year to go alone. This is your year, not mine."

John clamped his teeth together and went back to cleaning the rifle as, outside, the new flakes came down, roiling in the slight puffs of wind, taking life briefly as they slid past the window and hit the yellow glow from the lamp.

# FIVE

John awakened before the alarm went off and sat bolt upright in bed. It was opening morning, deer season, and the old ways had come back, the old excitement. At least for the moment.

He kicked out from under the quilt and put his feet on the floor, the cold floor. John had an upstairs room without heating grates and when the wood stove went down to a smolder in the kitchen, the upstairs cooled fast. He pulled on wool socks, thick ones his grandmother had knitted out of raw wool, and pulled his pants on over them with a scrape of cold cloth.

He could see his breath. *It must have dropped quite a bit during the night and that's good*, he thought. If it got down around zero and there was new snow it would be still and clear and that was good for hunting.

Downstairs he heard his grandmother moving about in the kitchen and he smiled. It was three in the morning—earlier than he normally got up, so he could do chores before he hit the woods—and it still didn't matter. He couldn't get up ahead of her, even if he tried. She always got up first and put coffee on the stove and had the fire going before he made it to the kitchen.

John pulled his shirt on and went downstairs, two steps at a time but quietly because he knew his grandfather would still be asleep. He was sleeping later now, and needing it.

In the kitchen he was assailed by smells. The tang of the pine kindling in the wood stove cut above everything, but it was mixed with the soft smell of bread warming on the warming rack and of raw potatoes frying with canned venison from the year before.

"Good morning." John's mouth was watering already. "Sure smells good in here."

"Morning." His grandmother smiled. "I'll have breakfast for you after chores."

John went to the door and pulled on his jacket. Outside he was met with a wall of cold. It was, he guessed, a little below zero—he could tell because the hair in his nose froze and stuck together—but it felt colder because he'd just come out of a warm room.

The rubber on his shoe pacs stiffened and the snow crunched as he walked to the barn in the dark.

Inside the barn it was warm, as always, and he quickly fed the cows and scraped the gutters and went back to the house for the buckets and separator parts while the cows were eating.

He was surprised to see his grandfather sitting at the kitchen table when he came back in. He was sipping a cup of hot coffee, the steam working up around his cheeks.

"Good morning," John said.

The old man nodded his greeting. "How are things in the barn?"

"Fine. Calves are all right, cows standing to

milk. I fed silage and hay. Grained the horses. I'm going back out to milk."

"You go ahead and milk and separate. I'll take it after that so you can hit the woods."

John hesitated. "Are you sure? There's plenty of time and I can just as easily do it all."

"No. It'll gray up in the east pretty soon and you want to be out by the swamp when it comes into light."

John nodded. That was right: hunt early, eat early is what they said. Hunt late, stand and wait. "All right. If you're sure."

"Absolutely. I'll be fine."

John went back out to the barn with all the buckets and got to milking. It was still pitch dark but some of the chickadees around the granary were starting to make morning sounds and it spurred him a bit.

Milking went well. Nobody kicked over any buckets or was froggy — hopping around — and he got through it without problems. Also, hunting had entered his mind and it kept him from thinking about his grandfather quite so much, took his thoughts away from bad things.

When he finished separating the milk and cream he carried the cream back to the house and left the milk in buckets for the calves. He debated about feeding the calves but his grandfather would have become angry and perhaps would have felt useless, and John didn't want that.

Outside, the morning was coming. John stopped halfway to the house and looked to the east. Not enough light yet to hunt, certainly—he couldn't see the front sight on the rifle—but it was coming.

He walked a little faster. Inside the kitchen, breakfast was on the table and he smiled. It amazed him how his grandmother always knew when he was coming in to eat. He could be out in the fields with the tractor, have a breakdown and walk in for a part and there would be food on the table when he walked in the door. She always knew. *She always knows everything*, he thought—*just quietly always knows everything there is to know.*

John asked her one evening how she knew so much. They were sitting in the kitchen, just the two of them, and John had been asking about his parents.

"I don't know that much about people," she said, flustering. But John could tell she was pleased by the question. "I just try to know as much as I can about something before I talk about it."

She'd gone on to tell John about his parents. Facts about them—how they looked, how they acted under certain conditions. And when she was done, John knew his parents in one way, her way, but he knew that it was honest knowledge.

When he thought of his grandmother that's the word that came to mind—honest. She was honest, and soft, and gentle. An honest, soft gentle person.

He set the cream in the cool-hole by the pump, where it would stay cool, but not freeze, until they went into town later in the week to sell cream, and hung his jacket up.

"I could eat a wolf," he said. "Raw."

His grandfather had been in the privy and he came in. "Set to food. I'll take care of the calves."

John nodded, glad that he had not fed the calves himself. It would have been wrong to take the work away from his grandfather—like saying he couldn't do it, somehow.

Clay went out and John washed at the pump and sat at the table. In the middle was a pile of fresh raw-fried potatoes and strips of venison; he loaded his plate. There was also syrup and he put some on the meat, sprinkled salt and pepper and started eating. He had learned about syrup on meat from Emil; it had looked bad at first, but when he tried it the taste was great. Especially on a cold morning.

"I set some aside for sandwiches for you, so you don't have to save any."

"What about Grandpa?"

"He's already had—just set to. You can't hunt hungry, especially if you hunt long."

She seemed different, somehow. Almost cheerful. Something he couldn't pin down but definitely something new had slipped into her actions.

The depression of the night before had vanished, almost as if a mist had left the house, and he ate heartily. Meat and potatoes with syrup was the best breakfast, better than pancakes any day, and he ate until he started to feel full and then stopped. Normally he would have gone past full and had food for all day, but when you hunt you want to hunt with a little edge on your belly—that's how his grandfather put it. Not hungry, but so the full feeling has worn off when you hit the woods—it makes it easier to see things. To shoot things.

When he'd finished eating John took his plate

to the sink and kissed his grandmother on the cheek and went to the entryway. There he put his coat on and a scarf and a wool hat and wool mittens Agatha had knitted. She brought two sandwiches wrapped in wax paper, which he slipped into his jacket pocket, and she handed him an apple with the other hand, a barrel apple from the basement, which he knew would be tangy and sweet at the same time.

The rifle was in the rack by the door and he took it down, as well as the box of shells from the shelf on the gun rack. John knew he wouldn't need the whole box so he just took out five cartridges, brassy and shiny with copper bullets tipped in silver, and dumped them in the top pocket of his jacket. He decided he would load in the woods.

He waited.

". . . It's going to be all right."

He thought about that and knew that she was wrong. It wasn't going to be all right. A part of him knew that his grandfather was going to end, end and be gone. But there was that small edge of hope in her voice, hope which she held the way a drowning person holds a stick. And John would not damage that hope, so he nodded and smiled. "I know, I know. I'll see you when I get back."

Outside, the cold hit him again, harder because he'd been in and his body had gotten used to the warm kitchen and the warm food. He felt it come in around his cuffs past the mittens, around the back of his neck.

By the barn he could see the glow from the lantern and he thought of going to say goodbye to his grandfather, but he would be busy and it would bother him.

Instead John wheeled left off the porch and walked straight north from the house across the pasture until he came to the trees that marked the edge of the woods.

Just inside the tree line he stopped and loaded the rifle, sliding the cartridges into the side-loading gate slowly, carefully. When all five were in the tube magazine he worked the lever once and brought a shell up into the chamber. Then he let the hammer down to the safety half cock and cradled the gun in the crook of his arm and paused, getting a feel for the morning and the woods.

It had stopped snowing and there was a gray light from false dawn coming off the snow. It still wasn't light enough for hunting, but close, very close, and he knew that by the time he reached the edges of the great swamp there would be enough light to see the sights of the rifle.

The woods were still. The new snow took down sound the way a blanket would, holding sound low and muffled, and with the freshness for tracking and the quiet it was nearly a perfect morning for hunting deer.

He turned his back on the farm and headed into the woods.

# SIX

John knew there were many ways to hunt deer. Some hunters drove them into other men who were posted with guns. Others walked around until they saw a deer and tried to shoot it. Still others picked a spot near a deer trail and stood and waited for a deer to come along.

And now and then a hunter would use the

stalking method—move quietly on fresh tracks and try to catch a deer off guard. This final method was very difficult to do successfully and demanded total concentration and complete knowledge of deer.

John used a combination of methods—he did some stalking and some standing. He would move through the woods as quietly as possible for a distance—perhaps a quarter of a mile—and then he would stop and stand for a time, usually half an hour or so.

He had learned it from his grandfather.

"You have to think deer," Clay had told him. "You have to think deer, you have to *be* deer inside your head. Be quiet, move quiet, and be deer."

The country he was hunting was very good deer country but hard to hunt. His grandfather's farm lay on the edge of a huge peat swamp-bog that covered all of northern central Minnesota. The bog extended over two counties, and in the spring and summer it was a mucky quagmire that had defied people forever. Ducks and geese nested there by the thousands; moose and timber wolves and deer lived on spruce "islands" that stuck above the level of the swamp.

It was not a place, in the summer, where life was easy. Even the deer and moose and small game had trouble. Deer were discovered wandering blind from the ravaging flies that chewed at their eyes, and moose had been found dead from loss of blood because of ticks.

But in the fall life comes to the swamp; relatively easy life. The bugs are down for the winter, the peat is frozen solid and the land becomes passable.

John's great grandfather had made his farm along the edge of this swamp. Far enough away to avoid the worst clouds of mosquitoes, close enough to get good soil. And while Clay had trouble now and then with wolves, the farm had easy access to good deer hunting.

The swamp was perfect cover for the raising of deer, for hiding fawns from wolves, and that was important. The wolves hunted deer, coursed through them, in the winter, like sharks hitting schools of fish.

When he was small and came across his first wolf kill, it had bothered John. When wolves killed it was usually in brutal fashion, at least by some human standards—a slow and tearing death. A pulling down and closing off of life.

But later John realized that there wasn't a

right or wrong way about wolves hunting and killing the deer. There was just the wolves' way. That was the way they were and had nothing to do with what man thought was right or wrong. John still didn't like it, but at least he thought he understood it and that helped him when he discovered the fawns the wolves had taken and torn to pieces.

But because the wolves were so active in the fall, the deer moved away from them and that meant they moved out of the swamp, which in turn meant that deer hunting became very good around the edges of the swamp. John now worked on the western edge. Or perhaps it might be best to say that he was at the edge of the edge, working in.

Around the outside there were huge hardwood forests that had once been logged off but were now coming back and they were mixed with stands of poplar and willows. The deer browsed in the willows when the snow got too deep for them to get at low plants, and John moved quietly through the willows, stooping and weaving, taking deliberate steps, stopping often to listen.

Deer are not silent. When they run through the willows in the fall and the willows are dry and hard it sounds like somebody tipping over a lumber cart.

But there was no sound this gray dawn and John decided the deer hadn't yet moved this far out of the swamp. Then, too, there were no new tracks in the fresh snow.

He worked slowly further into the edge of the swamp, hitting the deep grass and the open areas of the bog.

It was full light now, with the top edge of the sun slipping up over the tree line to the east. Tight cold had come down and he felt it working into his shoulders. He had just rezipped his jacket when he heard the noise.

It was a releasing sound, as if a branch or tree which had been held had been turned loose—a kind of *swoosh*—in back of him, back to his right, and he froze, waiting for another sound to guide him.

None came.

He turned and took two steps, then two more, and so covered a distance of perhaps thirty yards through the willows until he came to a deer bed.

It was about a yard across, where snow had melted down to bare swamp grass in a cupped little warm place under a stand of willows.

*Very cozy*, he thought. It almost looked inviting. He knelt next to the bed and felt the grass and it was still warm. That had been the sound. A deer had been here in its storm bed—John knew they holed up sometimes when it snowed—and he had walked past it and it had jumped up, apparently hitting the willow on the way.

It must have surprised the deer, his coming, because the first tracks were more than ten feet from the bed. The deer had bounded up and away. The next tracks were twenty feet from the first ones, out into a clearing and across, craters in the new snow where the deer had run.

*Well*, he thought. *I was close to one, anyway, even if I didn't know it.* He decided to follow the tracks, or work in the same direction as the deer.

*Better*, he thought, *to go after one you know is fresh than to hunt blind and hope.* It wasn't likely he'd see the deer soon, but it could happen and if it did he might get a shot and make meat early so he could get back and take care of work around the farm so his grandfather wouldn't have to.

It came to him suddenly that he hadn't thought about his grandfather for nearly an hour and he didn't know if that was good or if that was bad.

He brought his mind back around to the tracks.

There was a saying among the old-timers that you could either hunt deer or you could do something else. You could not do two things when it came to hunting deer—hunting required too much concentration.

John went back to hunting.

# SEVEN

In the clearings the snow hung on top of the matted swamp grass and it made hard going. His foot came down through the snow and then on past another eight inches to the peat beneath the grass. It was slow, stumbling work.

And in the willows he had to weave back and forth, so while it was easier walking—the grass was not so deep in the willows—it was still slow.

By midmorning he had only gone two miles, moving with the tracks. He had not seen the deer again but knew several things about it just the same. It was either a doe or a small buck—he could tell that by the size of the tracks, but he was not yet good enough to tell its sex. Older hunters could, but he wasn't sure of it; it had something to do with the way the foot came down.

He knew the deer wasn't unduly frightened. After he had jumped it out of the bed it had bounded for two hundred yards but then it had settled down to an even pace, just walking-running ahead of him easily. It wasn't panicking or running hard, the way deer did when the wolves got close.

He knew this deer was healthy. The steps were even, the weight came down evenly—it didn't limp or weave.

And he knew the deer wasn't a yearling, or a first-year fawn, which he wouldn't have shot even if he'd gotten a chance. His grandfather didn't kill first-year animals and he didn't either. If it had been a yearling it would have been all over the place, wandering as it fed, and probably running in spurts if it felt that it was being followed.

It wasn't until he reached one of the pine and spruce islands in the swamp that he came close to the deer again.

The island was about a hundred yards long, shaped in a large oval, and John worked across another clearing to get to it, wading through the snow-grass, stopping often to listen and watch.

It was easy to follow the tracks. The snow was all new and there didn't seem to be any other tracks in the area, except for rabbits. They had moved during the snow storm and left a patch-work of trails.

As he entered the pines on the island he stopped once more and listened, letting his eyes work ahead through the underbrush. It was like a make-believe land, what his grandmother would have called a fairy place; a place shot with silver and beauty.

The sun was as high as it was going to get now, an orb in the midsouth sky, and the light came down through the pines to make diamonds of the snow. Light sparkled all around, caught in the ice crystals as he stepped, showering his way with gold. He'd never seen anything like it and he looked down to see the snow move away from his legs in fire and when he looked up he saw her. A doe.

She had been in back of a spruce, all covered with snow and looking like a picture on a Christmas card and when he looked up she stepped out and saw him and was gone, that fast, but she left an image in his mind the way the snow had. When she jumped out from in back of the spruce the snow showered out and around and caught the fire from the sun and took the light to make her something other than what she was.

He held his breath. It had only lasted part of two seconds and yet he held his breath for half a minute, thinking of it. The rifle had come up of its own accord, settled against his shoulder, then gone down. There was no real time for a shot.

Then he breathed. It was over, over and gone and his breath came in a burst. He'd never seen anything like it. A shower of gold around a golden doe; beauty splashed through the woods.

After another minute he shook his head and continued. There was much beauty in the woods. His grandfather had told him the woods were *all* beauty. But that didn't change the basic fact: he had to make meat. They needed the food. And a doe was the best meat.

But something nagged at him, something he didn't understand. There was a mixing of things in his mind, or the start of a mixing that he couldn't quite pin down. As he walked the doe's tracks he started thinking of other things again; of his grandfather, of the way they lived, of what was coming for his grandfather. And the lines between the thoughts got blurred; the doe mixed with his grandfather and they both mixed with him.

He had to fight to concentrate on hunting.

He moved on.

As she left the spruce island, the doe had taken great bounds — twenty and thirty feet from print to print, the initial getaway jumps that all deer take when in danger, whether from man or wolf. But inside half a mile the tracks eased down and by the time John had followed another mile, through two more clearings and across two more spruce islands, she had calmed again.

It was when she'd settled into another bed that he finally got a chance to kill her.

# EIGHT

John had read several books about deer and deer hunting. One writer would say all deer do this, another would say all deer do that. But in truth the deer didn't read the books and they did just as they wanted.

Some deer slept at night and fed in the day, some bedded down during the day and fed at night. Still others slept and fed intermittently all day and all night. There was not a normal way for deer, John knew—only the deers' way.

The deer that John was following bedded often during the day. In a normal twenty-four hours she might make four or five beds—some in darkness, others during the warm part of the day where the sun could get her.

After her second near brush with John she went farther. She was not yet really alarmed, that much John could see from her tracks. They were still full of purpose, though for half a mile she stretched them out and covered distance with some speed.

By the time John was well into the first half mile of tracks the doe was two miles away. And this distance gave her time to get out of the escape mentality—he could see the tracks settle down, get steady.

In nature, John knew, danger came with great suddenness. A mouse could be feeding peacefully on a stem of grass one second and be in a fox's belly the next instant. Two grouse could be performing the mating ritual and within a heartbeat come under an owl's silent slashing attack.

But if danger comes suddenly it also leaves

quickly. If the fox misses the mouse, it seldom persists; the owl looks for another meal. It takes too much precious energy to chase food that is forewarned; it's much easier to find prey that can be taken without so much effort, off guard.

By the time she'd gone those two miles the doe had forgotten about John. Her tracks settled down and John followed them slowly, carefully.

He knew he could get her, knew by her tracks. She would move ahead of him and stay there for a time but she would forget and all he had to do was stay on the tracks and he would get a shot. And if he got a shot he would get her.

He visualized it. She would move and then stop and he would put the bullet through her shoulder and she would stagger sideways and down with the impact. The life would go out of her, out and out, leaving the gray film on her eyes and he would cut her throat and the red would flow out on the snow, warm and rich and steaming . . .

He shook his head. It was wrong to project when hunting. Nothing came the way it was supposed to come and planning didn't work. You might stand and watch a clearing for hours, waiting for the deer to come out, and it would pass ten feet in back of you and you wouldn't know it.

He washed his mind clear, took a mouthful of snow to wet his tongue and replace some of the moisture he was losing by perspiring. He was not warm, but he knew he was sweating into his clothes because that's what always happened when he worked in the winter.

It was noon now. The sun was peaking and he turned his face toward it as he walked, let the heat warm his cheeks. It would get cold tonight, very cold. Maybe fifteen or twenty below. He would have to be sure to get the doe early so he could start back. If he was out much after dark he would either have to keep moving or stop and build a fire and ride the cold out. He had matches and the sandwiches and his grandparents wouldn't worry. He knew how to handle himself in the woods—he'd had a good teacher in his grandfather. Still, he didn't relish the discomfort of standing over a fire all night.

He would get the doe early, he decided. Work a little harder and catch up, get a shot. He grunted a bit as he stepped over a windfall—a lare poplar the wind had torn out of the swamp, with a disk of roots sticking in the air. His leg came down and went through the deep snow and grass and threw him over at an angle, put him in an awkward position and he looked up and there she stood.

She had made a bed on the far side of the windfall where the sun could warm her, protected by the roots from any wind. John's eyes took it all in. The small cupped bed in the grass, still warm and steaming, the sudden flurry of movement, a blur of red-brown as she got up and the freeze, the freeze as she stood.

John was leaning to his left and while it threw him slightly off balance to stand that way, it did not keep him from being able to use the rifle.

She stood frozen, eyes wide open, staring at him. He'd caught her somehow, off guard. He was on top of her and she panicked and froze and stood now, stood waiting for death.

The rifle came up, floated up to his shoulder in a fluid movement, a movement he'd known many times. It happened with great speed but he visualized it always in slow motion; the rifle coming up, his thumb pulling the hammer back, the bead of the front sight nestling into the sloping buckhorn of the back, the bead coming perfectly to rest on the doe's shoulders where, in back of the hair and muscle, he knew the heart pulsed, pumping, beating.

His finger tightened on the trigger and that, too, was automatic, all part of the same motion, all natural and flowing. The gun up and the hammer back and the sights on target, on her heart, on her death and his finger squeezing and squeezing the trigger to give her that death, to blow her over and down and make her into meat.

But he didn't shoot.

The moment hung for hours, burned into him, became part of him. The doe standing side-on to him, so close he could see her hairs, eyes wide and clear, little puffs of steam from her nose, a twitch in her back leg from a ready muscle held in check. All of it seen over the blue black of the rifle barrel. Two seconds that lasted hours.

*Just pull the trigger*, he thought. *Pull it and let the sear drop and that will let the hammer fall and set off the primer which will ignite the powder and send the bullet out to take her life.*

His finger was tight on the trigger, knuckle tense and white under the mitten.

But he didn't shoot.

*Why am I not shooting? We need the meat and there it is and I've hunted this deer to give her death and make her meat and it's all here for me, for us, and still I don't pull the trigger. Why?*

The doe moved.

Her back foot lifted and stepped forward a couple of inches and settled into the snow again but her head was still.

*It's the same doe*, he thought suddenly, finger still tight on the trigger. *It's the doe from the other night.*

And with that thought came another one: *She knows me.*

*She remembers me from the stoneboat and spreading manure and the horses that night. She knows who I am and that's why she isn't running, isn't trying to leave.* And he knew that had she moved at first he would have fired and killed her, and he knew that it was getting harder and harder to kill her.

Knowing her made it hard to finish the trigger squeeze and having her know him made it still harder, and still the moment hung, suspended — time in the cold — frozen time.

He had not breathed for twenty seconds now and more, holding only half a breath, and he let it out in a burst that made an explosive sound.

"*Whewwwgh!*"

She jumped. With no gathering of muscle she exploded up and away and came down thirty feet to the side in a great burst of snow and then two more bounds and she was out of sight and gone.

And still he did not shoot.

The snow was still hanging in the air, drifting down like traces of white flour when he lowered the rifle, staring after her, seeing the image of her still, etched in his eyes: the doe standing and the rifle sights on her — and he not shooting.

It made no sense.

He was still leaning over the windfall in a bad position. It took him a few seconds to get his leg loose and drag it over the log, then another two or three to brush the snow off his leg and clean out the top of his boot and when he looked back down the trail he thought he saw the outline of her standing in the willows. He couldn't be sure but he saw the markings of a deer in the vertical gray, caught in the sun, and then it was gone.

He shook his head. Part of all this didn't make sense. Why should he not shoot, and why should she stand to him, stand for death that way?

John looked around, as if trying to see the answer, then up at the blue sky and down at the rifle in his hands and then he started to walk.

He followed her trail in the new snow, followed the part of her that was left behind.

He did not know why.

He knew that he hadn't shot her, and he knew he had wanted to shoot her and that made no sense, no sense at all. He did not understand himself, did not know what made him hold the death back. But there was something later for him, something later on down that he wanted to see, to hear, to feel.

It all meant more than just the deer and the gun and him. It meant something bigger that he couldn't understand just yet.

That's what he thought, anyway. But another part of John told him that he was following her because he really had no choice. He could not hunt another deer having failed on this one, and he could not turn and go home because it was not a finished thing.

He followed the doe's tracks because at that time that was all there was for him—the tracks leading off into the snowy woods.

The tracks called him and he followed.

# NINE

He could see the fear in her now.

He was following her and the fear drove her and she ran hard; long and deep in the first burst the way she would have run to get away from wolves — she ran for her life.

John followed the tracks easily, not hurrying. He still wasn't quite sure why he was staying with her, tracking her, but he kept going for another hour and a half to cover the same distance she had covered in eight and a half minutes.

Speed was everything to her, to all deer. When mortal danger threatened the only recourse was speed, burning speed, speed that tore energy from the center of the deer and used her up.

She ran that way now. Ran from the danger of John and while she had paused long, too long, in the freeze position, she made up for it by now getting as much distance as possible in the shortest possible time between her body and the man with the gun.

But running long and hard burned her out. It showed in her tracks, a slight wobble now and then from running past her short-range endurance. She would have to rest soon, he knew, would have to bed down.

John knew this from hunting and from talking with his grandfather and other old hunters. There were stories of men who had taken time and walked deer down and John had always figured they were just that, stories. But he knew that deer had a short burn, nonetheless, and that was in his mind now as he followed her tracks.

The tracks.

The tracks were her and they were more, too. They were small stories in the snow. At first, when she ran scared from him she had torn the snow and left diamonds scattered in the sun across the white. But when she settled down again and began looking for a place to rest, the tracks were more controlled, her feet almost inserted in the snow, with no splashing.

He knew her from the tracks. Knew more about her all the time and kept going at first for that, he thought: to learn more about her, to try and find what it was that made her stick in his mind. She was there already, as if she'd been there before he came hunting.

The second time he got her up she didn't freeze but made off to the left, the north, in a smooth, low run. He could easily have hit her. She started forty yards away and he had a good sixty- or seventy-yard run to get the sights on her but he didn't even raise the rifle.

He cut the corner and again picked up her tracks and started following once more. Again there was panic in the tracks, the long burst, but he knew he wouldn't lose her, because it was all new snow and there were no other deer and it was clear and there wouldn't be any more snow to cover her tracks.

*I'll follow for a while*, he thought, having used up all the reasons and excuses. *Maybe I can still kill her and take liver for Grandpa. Maybe I can make her into meat*, he thought, knowing that something about that was wrong. *Maybe I'll just stay with her. I'll follow for a while and see what happens.*

The sun was moving toward evening now. It was still well above the southwestern horizon, but it would drop fast and when it did it would get dark. John frowned, trying to remember the moon. Finally he remembered that it would be nearly full so there would be good night light. Sometimes when there was new snow and the moon was full he could almost read at night.

He took a sandwich from his pocket and tore the paper off while walking. His first bite tasted so good that it made his jaws ache but on the second one he remembered that it was a venison sandwich and the meat seemed to take on a taint, not so much a bad taste as a bad feeling.

He did not take a third bite but put the sandwich back in his pocket and instead ate the apple. When he was finished he threw the core away and kept walking, always walking.

He was tiring now, but not exhausted. The calves of his legs ached slightly now and then and his stomach hurt a bit from stepping over the swamp grass, but it was nothing to him yet and he walked easily.

*I'll bet*, he thought, *I could track her all night. I'll bet I could just keep going in the moonlight and stay on her tracks and then . . .*

He did not know what came next. Just *and then . . .*

He was halfway through a stand of jack pine on a small sand island in the sea of swamp grass when dark caught him.

John knew that starting in November for four months dark hammers down fast in the north. In literally minutes it goes from day to dark night, so fast it catches things. Dark can catch a rabbit in a clearing, letting a fox find him. It catches mice in the open and lets owls have them.

And it caught John.

He stopped then, studied the sky and the terrain. There were times when he was young when he would have worried—being caught in the dark miles from home in a strange woods. But not now. He could see the stars, see the polestar, and though it was cold, the wind had also died so the cold didn't blow in.

And there was the moon. The moon would be south, go to bed in the southwest. "You're never lost when you can see the sun and the stars and the moon," his grandfather had told him. The moon was a pale-blue light that took life from the snow and changed the dark to just a different kind of day, not night at all, so John wasn't lost.

The tracks shone in the moonlight, called to him from the inside, and he started walking again, following.

At first, while he worked the tracks and went deeper and deeper into the swamp he saw other things, saw beauty.

He moved to within fourteen inches of a snowshoe rabbit, frozen in the moonlight like a white ghost, caught by surprise while playing fox-and-geese. John could not tell where the snow ended and the rabbit began; the rabbit was a part of the whiteness.

A timber wolf followed him for a short time, until John turned in a clearing and saw him. The wolf had been looking for mice and for a time John thought he might be after the doe and it angered him and he made a sound in his throat.

It was an animal sound—a sound that wasn't a sound. It came from inside some way, from a pit that he didn't understand. It was a sound for the wolf, a warning for the wolf—a thing that went out from John, out to the wolf.

He did not want to kill the doe. He didn't want

the wolf to do it either and he was glad when the wolf turned away, not in fear, but just naturally.

*She is not mine*, he thought, stopping suddenly, *but she is of me now, somehow; I will follow her for a while and we shall see.*

*I will follow her for a while and I will touch her.*

The thought came like a fast wind, working around the sides of his brain into the middle.

*I will follow her and I will touch her and she will be mine then, mine without me having to kill and give her death and make her meat.*

*But why?* He had never thought like this before. He was tired now — had been tracking for twelve hours, moving steadily, getting the deer up and pushing her ahead, often without seeing her. But he wasn't odd-tired yet, just tired — and yet he wanted to touch the doe.

He *would* touch her.

He would stay on the trail until she couldn't get away from him anymore, stay and stay and when he caught her he would touch her.

*And if I do that*, he thought, *if I can follow her and touch her without giving her death then death will be cheated.*

*If I touch the deer.*

He looked to the moon again and saw that it

was indeed full and there would be good light all night and he started walking.

There was purpose now, an aim. He thought suddenly that it would be better to dump the rifle, to leave it hanging in the branches of a tree. He would pick it up on the way back, if he came this way. If not he'd come out on his tracks and get it later. It was of steel and heavy and meant death and he didn't want to carry it any further. It did not fit with the doe any longer, or with him, and when he put it in the tree he felt a weight lifting from him that was out of proportion to the four pounds the rifle weighed. It was a weight from his thoughts. An extra part was gone, a part that didn't matter. Now there was just John and the doe and the night and the tracks, and he fought the tiredness away and kept going. He picked up the stride and worked to increase the pace.

He did not come to see how the deer was his grandfather, or the spirit of his grandfather's life, until later in the night, almost daylight the next morning.

And by then nothing was the same as it had started out to be. The deer wasn't a deer anymore and he wasn't John Borne anymore, either. Everything was changed.

# TEN

Through the night he moved, weaving amongst
the willows, flowing across the clearings, following her tracks, watching the doe change from a
deer to something more and something less.

She went mad in the night. She ran too hard
and went down and fell and he saw the splotch in
the snow where it had happened and at first he

smiled, some part of him felt good that he had caused her to run, but then it changed to sadness and he hoped that she would not do that again, would not panic and fall and perhaps hurt herself. But she ran in jerks through the night, great tearing runs that took her energy.

She ran across clearings and amongst the willows and pine, away, away—always away from the sound of the steps that kept coming.

And John in some ways became less than he was before—less the hunter, less the man tracking her—and in some ways he became more than he was before. He took strength from the snow and the winter and the beauty of the night, took power from the moon and the white light and kept going.

More than once he fell asleep while he was walking. From three in the morning on to daylight he had a terrible time staying awake. His legs and body kept on but his mind and spirit went out and he dropped, face down in the snow, and it was hard to get up.

Once he simply lay and felt the sleep come and knew that if he didn't get up the sleep might let him freeze, but he still couldn't move and wouldn't have moved except that he heard the deer.

The deer.

He heard her move in the red willows in the white light and he looked and saw her and she was afraid but she was somehow beckoning, too. The sound pulled him and he got up and stood on his feet and started walking again.

In the night he changed.

In the night he changed from following the deer to becoming the deer. A part of him went out to the deer and a part of the deer went out of her into him, across the white light and he wasn't the same. He would never be the same again. He was of the deer and the snow and the night and he kept himself but he lost his spirit and gained a new one.

> *I am not*
> *but I am.*
> *I am the deer.*

It became a chant, a song that he did not sing aloud but which still went out before him down the line of tracks to the deer and he hoped she knew the song, knew the beauty of the song and knew that he meant her no harm.

But she could not know.

She could know only that this man kept following, stayed on her trail the way no wolf would have done, spent energy the way no predator would have done, stayed and stayed and stayed until the fear was alive in her.

Big-eyed terror. She was tiring in the night, her muscles quivering. She ran in bursts ahead of John, ran until she was out of sight and then went down in the grass to rest, but always the steps kept coming.

In panic, in a clearing, she voided all her fluids and solid waste in a small pile that lay steaming in the snow, sinking, and she ran on.

John came upon the pile and it was still hot, still giving off airs and he knelt to smell it. He could taste the smell, acid on the sides of his tongue, and he looked up and he knew her from the smell and the taste, knew that no other deer would have that smell or taste and even if he lost the trail now he could go by smell and that wasn't the same. That made him different. He couldn't smell that way before and that made him part of the doe. He would stay on her, keep after her until he owned her. No, more than that, more than owning.

He would touch her and touch himself and

touch his grandfather's spirit and touch death and he would win.

It was all with the doe, all of it—and he loved her.

He would touch her, and he loved her. Loved her deeply—what she was and the way she looked and what she meant. She had brought him out, danced before him in the winter, danced and pulled him into the swamp. Part of him said that it couldn't be, but another part of him knew that the doe had come for him at the barn—come for him and danced him away.

In the night he was crazy, a little, and some of it came from being tired and some of it from thinking about his grandfather. The craziness came in short flashes and mixed with being not crazy so he couldn't tell the difference. And he didn't care.

The gray of false dawn showed him closer to the doe. He could see her now, see her often. Her bursts of running, open mouthed and hard, stretched only two hundred yards and he saw her moving ahead in the willows and across the clearings, looking back in fright, spit dripping from her tongue out the side of her mouth.

The deer.

And when full light came he hated himself as much as he loved the deer. She was running until her front legs collapsed, running until she caved in, and she plowed down into the snow and then up, staggering, to run again and he hated himself for driving her that way but he couldn't stop, couldn't make himself stop now.

He must touch her.

He must own her.

He must own-love-touch the doe and when that happened his grandfather would not die.

# ELEVEN

He had tracked her all that first day and all of that night, following in the moonlight and the new clean snow and through the next morning, and when the sun was highest his brain did not work right anymore.

He was tired beyond bearing, tired beyond the doe, weaving and staggering and falling and still not stopping. By midday there was nothing for him but the doe and the touching of the doe and it was no longer possible to distinguish between what was real and what was not.

Once in the morning light he watched the doe ahead of him and saw her turn and swore there was a light around her head. The light moved with her neck movements, was not a halo so much as a glow that came from within the doe and it was still there even when he wiped his eyes. The light stayed for five or six minutes and did not disappear until the doe staggered into some willows and was lost from sight.

Again, later, he was looking at the doe and it seemed that everything he saw in front of him was a mirror. Seemed that the doe was actually in back of him and that everything that was going to happen had already happened in back of him. It made his mind whirl and then his vision fogged and he fell down and would have stayed down again but for the doe.

She moved and he followed.

By noon she could not run but seemed to fall forward, fall away from him and just keep falling, with her legs catching up only to fall again for miles and miles.

And he came the same way. John was falling and making his legs catch up—he did not feel tired anymore, didn't feel anything.

At one in the afternoon he began seeing the doe all the time. She was blown out completely and could not even make the pretense of running. Instead she worked just to stay ahead of him, just ahead, always in sight—never more than a hundred yards, often less then fifty.

He saw her.

At one point she vomited from stress and there was some blood in it, blood mixed with bits of bark fiber from the last time she'd eaten, over a day before, and when he came on it he was sickened and felt the bile rise and he, too, vomited.

The air was warm and he hung his jacket over a bush, stuck his cap in his back pocket and poured sweat still. The sun was full on his back now as he worked north and he made sounds that weren't human, yet weren't animal—sounds from his throat as he watched her stagger and fall away from him, first to the left and then to the right.

At last when she went down she didn't get up as fast and then each time she fell she was slower to get up and he kept coming.

Coming—until there came a time when he was nearly on her before she got up, only to fall again, and then she didn't get up.

She was blown. Her ribs heaved for air as his did, her eyes showed edges of red, her mouth was open and her tongue stuck out to the side and he thought he'd never seen anything so awful and ugly and beautiful at the same time.

The doe was his and he didn't have to kill her, give her death, and he moved forward to her, on his hands and knees now, crawling, lunging, and she jerked to get away once and fell and he saw it as a picture, the doe on her side, heaving air, the yellow in the snow where she urinated in fear, the fear and the madness around her, the wild eyes, and he reached out and he touched her.

He was there and his hand went out and he touched her and then he fell, down and down in the snow and when he opened his eyes in a minute, an hour, a lifetime, she was gone.

He got up and stood, weaving, looking back on his trail. The sun was afternoon hot and he had touched her and she was gone, gone, but he had done it.

He knew because the yellow was still on the

snow and there were flecks of blood from her nostrils and the imprint of her muzzle in the white.

He had touched her.

And now he had to get home and tell his grandfather that he had done it, he had won and there would be life now—life taken from death. Life taken back.

# TWELVE

It was dark again when John reached the farm, dark and cold. He stopped in the woods on a small rise and looked at the house.

He couldn't tell his grandfather what had happened—at least not all of it. He had been chewing on it since he'd left the doe, walking all day in a thought haze. She had run in great loops and circles of fear but not a terrible distance from the farm. When he'd regained some of his thoughts he knew where he was and took a straight line back to the rifle and from there home — a seven-hour walk.

Seven hours of wondering what he would say to his grandfather and now the time had come. He would have to say something but he couldn't tell him of cheating death — that wouldn't work either.

The doe had taught him much, not about death but about life. And yet it was not something he could share with anybody — it was not something he was sure he really understood himself. It was just a thing that *was* — a way for something to be. She made him see a new way, but he could not make others do the same. They had to have their own deer.

His legs were on fire and the pain seemed worse now that he was close to home. He staggered down to the porch and leaned the rifle in the corner and stomped clear of snow and went in.

They were sitting at the kitchen table, just as they always sat. Relief flooded his grandfather's face, a clearing away of wrinkles, but he said nothing.

His grandmother coughed and cleared her throat, and he could see mist in the corners of her eyes, small tears.

"We were worried," she said, controlling her voice. "It came on to being long—longer than you've ever been at hunting."

John shook his coat off and hung it up and sat at the table, still silent.

"For all that you didn't make meat?" His grandfather lit his pipe, making clouds of smoke. He only smoked when he wanted to think before talking, he'd once told John. "Two days and some and no meat?"

John studied him. "It's not like it was before . . ." He trailed off, said nothing more for a long minute.

"What isn't? What's changed?"

*And that's it*, John thought, the idea searing across the front of his mind—*what has changed?* Had touching the deer altered anything? Was there not still death—still death coming to his grandfather?

"I . . . I found a doe and I followed her," he started, but it wasn't coming out right.

"For two days you followed a doe? And you didn't get a shot?"

John looked out the window yet could see nothing but the reflected room. The tablecloth with the pattern, the glow of the lamp—it was like another world facing the world he was in. A world that was the same and yet the opposite and he wished he were in the mirror world.

"A thing changed," John said. "A thing changed in hunting, in everything, and I walked after her but didn't shoot her."

His grandparents said nothing, waited.

"And I walked for two days and then I touched her. Actually two days, and a night. And when I touched her everything changed—everything about the way we are and what's happening."

He finished lamely, letting it simply end. His grandmother took a plate of meat and potatoes from the oven and put it in front of him. She had known somehow that he was coming because it wasn't stale food, still fresh. Or maybe she'd just kept a different plate warm each night. *No*, he thought, *she'd known somehow—just as she always knows.*

His grandfather put his pipe down. He never smoked when anybody was eating. He looked at John, then out the window. "You touched her? You really touched a live deer?"

John nodded. "I walked and walked and touched her. She couldn't get up."

Another long pause.

"Ain't that something, Aggie?" his grandfather

said. "He walked one down. Ain't that something?"

And there was a thing in his voice that John had never heard before. A touch of pride, perhaps; a building of something.

"I'll take that with me," his grandfather went on. "That's something I'll just take with me."

John had a forkful of meat halfway to his mouth and he stopped, put the fork down. He was surprised to see that his grandfather was crying, crying as he looked at his reflection in the window — or just looked out the window — and two thoughts cut through the tiredness in his mind, burned into his brain.

The first was that his grandfather was going to die. He would die and there was nothing John could do about it — nothing touching the doe could do about it. Death would come.

And the second thing was that death was a part of it all, a part of living. It was awful, a taking of life, but it happened to all things, as his grandfather said, would happen to John someday. Dying was just as much a part of Clay Borne as living.

"Tomorrow, I do the chores," John said. "You take it easy."

After that there was just the food and keeping his eyes open until he went up the stairs to bed where he dreamt of the doe and his grandfather and awakened in sweat when the dream became too real.

But he made no sound and went back to sleep evenly, even thoughts of the doe washed from his mind.